STO

D1220705

CREATIVE
EDUCATION

young
romance
books

Survival Camp!

by Eve Bunting

illustrated by Robert Gadbois

CREATIVE EDUCATION
CHILDRENS PRESS

Published by Creative Educational Society, Inc., 123 South Broad Street, Mankato, Minnesota 56001.
Copyright © 1978 by Creative Education, Inc. International copyrights reserved in all countries. No part of this book may be reproduced in any form without written permission from the publisher. Printed in the United States.
Library of Congress Cataloging in Publication Data
Bunting, Anne Eve.
Survival Camp.
SUMMARY: Survival camp is not Mimi's idea of a vacation but she is determined to meet its challenges.
(1. Survival — Fiction. 2. Camping — Fiction)
I. Title
PZ7.B91527Sv (Fic) 77-10681
ISBN 0-87191-631-2
Distributed by Childrens Press, 1224 West Van Buren Street, Chicago, Illinois 60607

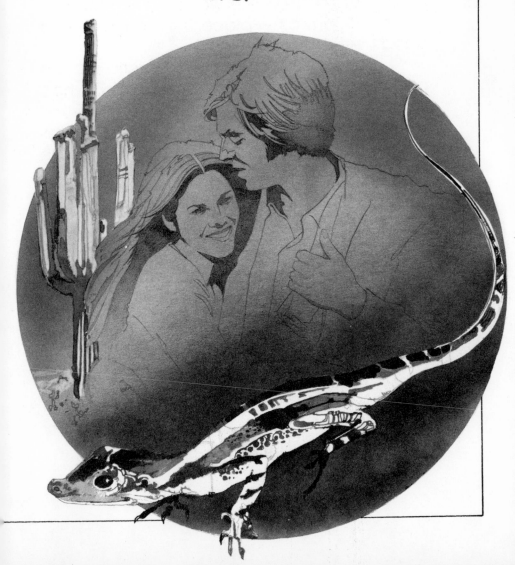

The truck had dumped them off in the middle of the scrubby Utah desert. The smell of its exhaust still hung in the morning air.

Mimi looked around at the other campers. There were twenty-four of them all together, sixteen boys and eight girls. It was a division of numbers she would have liked any other time, any other place. But nothing looked good here.

Survival camp! How in the world did she get stuck with this? Because her parents had sent her, that was why.

"Have you been to one of these camps before?" The boy standing next to her asked. He had red hair, freckles and a friendly grin.

"No," Mimi said. "Have you?"

His grin widened. "Yeah. Last year. I like punishment. By the way, my name's Red."

"I'm Mimi. You must have liked it then. Camp, I mean."

"I sure did. But then, I'm weird. You'll find out."

Great, Mimi thought. The resentment that had been simmering in her boiled up and over. Why had her parents done this awful thing to her? Their reasoning was all fouled up. Just because last year her brother Dave had car trouble in the desert and had to walk out.

Mimi's mother had wept. "If that had been you, Mimi, you'd be dead."

Dave smiled through cracked lips. "Our Mimi would be sitting there still, waiting for someone to carry her home. Somebody male."

"I would not either," Mimi said indignantly. "Besides, I'm not going to be making any dumb desert trips."

She couldn't believe it when her father had produced the Survival Camp booklet three days later.

"Don't you think this is going a bit far?" she'd asked. "Look, we live in San Francisco. I'll never need to camp out on Market Street. And there are plenty of coffee shops around. I'll never have to live off the land on Van Ness Avenue." Her sarcasm went right over their heads.

"Your mother and I have talked about it," her dad said. "There are things about you. . ." He'd stopped and Mimi had seen the looks her parents exchanged.

Her throat was suddenly dry. Did her dad know about the algebra test? Had Mr. Sommers told after all? He'd promised not to if she'd promise not to cheat again.

"You give up too easily," her dad went on. "Unless something's handed to you on a plate you don't even want it."

"She never has any trouble getting stuff handed to her," Dave butted in. "All Mimi has to do is bat her eyelashes and show her dimples. I swear, if a shark attacked her, Mimi would try making up to him before she tried swimming."

"Why don't you clam up?" Mimi said.

"We didn't ask for your opinion, Dave," their dad said. "Nevertheless." He plunked the ad for the Survival Camp down in front of Mimi. "We've registered you for the June session."

Mimi read aloud. "The wilderness values are the true values. Sleeping under the stars. Learning the meaning of independence and self-worth." She'd rolled her eyes in despair. "You've got to be kidding."

But they hadn't been kidding, and now she was here. She'd known it would be nauseating and it looked as if she'd been right.

One of the three camp counselors stepped forward. There were three counselors all together, two boys and this girl. They were all about twenty.

'I'm Sue," the girl said. "I want to give out your food packs." She went around handing over a small sack to each camper. "Check them out," she said. "You should have one potato, one carrot, one block of cheese, a bag of dried milk, one of flour, one of oatmeal, one of rice and one of brown sugar, and seven bouillon cubes. OK?"

"You can't mean it," someone wailed. "This is all? For ten days?"

Sue smiled. "You'll be glad there's not more by the time you've carried it a while. It gets to feeling pretty heavy. Besides, these are only supplementary rations. The desert is full of game and edible plants."

"Is there a pizza place?" someone else yelled.

One of the other counselors held up a hand. "Let's get our packs on and start hiking," he said. Mimi read the tag on his blue work shirt. Brad Taylor. His hair was thick and black as an Indian's and his eyes were the same blue-grey of the shirt, pale against his brown skin. His eyes moved from face to face, sizing them up. His glance seemed to pause when it came to Mimi. Oh, oh, she thought. This is the boss man. This is the one to look out for. This is the one who could smooth the way for me if I could get him on my side. She smiled, but there was no answering smile. The pale eyes narrowed, moved on.

From somewhere Mimi seemed to hear Dave's voice. "Showing your dimples isn't going to work, sis dear. This one's a shark. Start swimming."

Shut up, Dave, she told him.

"Let's walk," Brad Taylor said.

They walked. And they walked. Through scrub grass and brush. Up sandhills and down sandhills. With every step the sun grew hotter, the pack heavier. Mimi's boots rubbed her heels. The water in her canteen that was supposed to last all day was finished before the noon break.

She was walking in a daze and stumbled over the camper ahead of her when at last Brad called a halt.

She sprawled under a tree and closed her eyes. A tall glass of Coke floated in her mind. Ice chimed with the tinkle of temple bells. A small crescent of lemon was tilted on the glass rim, all glittering and juicy.

She sat up and licked her dry lips. When she screwed the cap of her canteen and tipped the bottle, only one tepid drop fell on her tongue.

"Here." A freckled hand reached a canteen in her direction.

"Oh, Red! You're saving my life. Honest." She had her fingers curled around the bottle neck when another hand came out of nowhere. This one was brown and thin and she knew who it belonged to without ever looking up. There they were, the three, overlapping, bodiless hands. The freckled one let go.

Mimi tugged.

The brown hand held on, the grip tightening until the nails were white.

3 1833 04380 4159

10

Mimi pulled with all her strength. "Let go," she gasped. "Just let go."

"You let go," a cold voice said.

"Will not!" Through her anger she heard the spoiled-rotten whine and she was transported back to kindergarten, struggling with a little curly haired boy for possession of the Crayola box. She remembered that she'd bitten him good and he'd let go. It had been a long since she'd had to bite a boy to get what she wanted but the temptation was strong now.

Brad was prying her fingers away, jerking the canteen out of her reach.

Mimi scrambled up. "Give that back. It's Red's." She glared through the sun and tree shadows.

"You drank your water," Brad Taylor said. "If you're thirsty that's your tough luck. Today you do without. Tomorrow you'll remember that it has to last the whole day." He gave the canteen to Red. "And you should know better, Red. This is a training process, a discipline. We talked about it before we started."

"Sorry, Brad," Red muttered.

Mimi licked her lips. "Aw come on, Brad. I'm awfully thirsty."

"I'm sure you are."

Nothing in the world had ever maddened her as much as his polite, disinterested face. She wanted to batter her fists against his chest and claw at his Indian brown skin.

"See that bush over there?" Brad asked quietly. "Those are edible berries. There's juice in berries."

"But I'm tired. I don't want. . . I want to lie down. . . ."

Brad shrugged. "Well then, I guess you're not all that thirsty."

Mimi leaned wearily against the tree trunk and watched him walk away. Of all the hateful things in this hateful camp, he was the worst. She closed her eyes against the sting of tears. How was she going to stand it?

In the days that followed they learned how to start fires using flint and steel, how to find edible plants and roots, how to get directions from sun shadows by day and from stars by night. They learned how to find water where animals had scratched or where cattails and willows grew. They learned how to make sun shelters and rain shelters, and Mimi learned to ration out her day's water, and not to ask for help because there was no one to help her. Everyone was too busy helping himself, just staying fed and dry and warm. She learned not to whine because there was no one to listen, and not to cry to go home, because she couldn't go home until camp was over, and she couldn't drop out because there was no place to drop to. This was it and there was nothing to do but struggle on.

When she woke up on the fourth day, Mimi knew she couldn't walk that day and wouldn't. Not for nobody or anything. There had to be a way to fake something.

She thought about it and called Sue over. Sue had been softer than the other two counselors, which Mimi thought was strange. Usually, where she was concerned, guys were the easy ones to handle.

"I've got the worst cramp in my leg," she told Sue. It was true anyway. She had the worst cramps everywhere. Her legs ached. So did her feet and her arms and her neck. Sometimes it seemed that even her teeth were exhausted.

Sue went for Harry, the other counselor, which wouldn't have been so bad except that Harry called over Brad.

They stood around Mimi as she sat on a sun-warmed rock trying to look sincere.

Harry rolled down her knee sock and massaged her calf.

Mimi gasped and squinched up her face.

"Feel any knots?" Sue asked.

Harry shook his head. "Should we stop for a while, Brad? It'll throw the schedule off for the truck pickup if we do."

"I don't think we need to stop," Brad said slowly. "We'll use a travois. It's the way Indians used to move their wounded."

You should know, Mimi thought. She watched as they cut down two poles and tied a blanket, stretcher-style between them. She hobbled across and lay in the blanket, hugging to herself the thought of one day, one blessed day without moving.

This time Dave's remembered voice whispered, "waiting for someone to carry you again, huh?"

Bug off, Dave, she told him. Mind your own darn business. She put her bedroll under her head and lay back.

"I'll take the first turn," Harry offered, picking up one end of the poles.

"No," Brad said. "I will."

Didn't they need two?

Mimi gazed up at the cloudless blue sky. The day might even be pleasant. She could have a nap.

The travois began to move.

"Ow," Mimi yelled. "What are you doing?"

Brad was dragging her, that's what he was doing. Dragging her! There must have been a hundred sharp, pointed rocks on the ground and each one stabbed at her through the blanket.

"Something wrong?" Brad's head turned but his feet kept on going.

"I'm. . . I'm. . ." The words came out in rattling spurts.

"I can't hear you."

Mimi held on to the edges of the blanket and peered around it. She was in time to see Brad turn away from a smooth patch of ground and head for a rock strewn stretch and she knew what he was doing. He was making the ride harder on purpose, because he knew. He knew.

There was one gigantic boulder and Brad was heading straight for it.

"Hey," Mimi yelled. She let herself slide off the blanket and thump on to the ground. She stood up and dusted off her legs and her blue shorts.

The travois had stopped moving. Brad stared down at her. There was a look in his eyes that she didn't understand but she knew she didn't like it.

"Leg cramps better?" he asked.

Mimi nodded.

"Think you can walk now?"

She nodded again.

Brad untied the blanket, shook it off and jammed it into his back pack. He strode away so suddenly that Mimi had to grab her bedroll and run to catch up or get left behind.

"You sure are a quick healer," Brad said over his shoulder and Mimi felt an anger and hatred stronger than she'd ever felt before. Who did he think he was?

She trudged along behind him. His shoulder muscles moved easily under his white T shirt. The Indian black hair lay thick and glossy against the brown of his neck. Mimi shivered. She felt like she was catching pneumonia. It froze up here at night. She wished she didn't have to walk behind Brad, like some old-time Indian squaw. She wished she didn't have to look at him, because to look at him was to have to think about him and that was something she could do without.

Red had told her Brad was nineteen. He'd been counseling at these camps for three summers. What kind of a freak would want to spend the whole summer up here? Red said Brad was an Environmental Studies major in college and that he lived in Chicago. Mimi really hadn't wanted to know all that stuff, but there was no way to turn Red off. So. . .maybe she had asked a question or two. She'd never come up against a guy like Brad before so it was kind of interesting to try to figure out what made him tick.

He stopped so abruptly in the path that she bumped into him.

"Sorry," she muttered, more conscious of the white T shirt against her face than she'd ever been of anything before. What is the matter with me, she thought. This wilderness living is driving me wacko.

Brad took hold of her wrist and nodded to a rock where a small, green lizard hung motionless. It glittered and sparkled, unreal and beautiful as a jewelled pin.

It's. . ." Mimi began.

"Sh!"

Mimi looked up into Brad's face. There was a softness in it, a tenderness that was almost love. She caught her breath.

He bent over and flicked the little, pointed tail with a gentle finger.

The lizard scampered in a streak of color over the bulge of the rock. Its tail streaked the dirt, and then it was gone.

Brad let go of her wrist and she rubbed the place where his fingers had been.

Walking again behind him she tried to sort out what she'd seen. The way he'd looked at

that lizard. The way he'd looked at her, earlier,
when she got off the travois. The way he'd felt
had been there in his eyes. Love for the lizard,
contempt for her. She wondered if there was a
girl in Chicago that Brad gifted with the lizard
look. Poor, dumb girl. She probably spent half of
her life just waiting for that heart-melting gaze.
Poor, dumb girl.

Brad and Red each shot a rabbit the next day with their bows and arrows and there was a rabbit stew for dinner. It tasted terrific.

After they'd eaten, they crowded around the campfire and sang a bunch of old, sappy songs, accompanied by Sue on her harmonica. Red sat next to Mimi and held her hand. The stars were out, hanging like crystals from the chandelier of the sky. Somebody saw a satellite passing, its light glowing down on them from thousands of miles away. On the other side of the fire Brad sat, cross-legged, whittling a stick. The flames glinted on his face, turning it to the color of a new penny.

Mimi sighed and lay back, staring into the sky that went up and up for ever. There was a contented feeling inside her and she tried to analyze it. The rabbit stew, of course. It was nice to be full for a change. But there was something else. She was pretty pleased with herself. Tonight she'd been the one to start the fire and Harry had complimented her.

"Doing better there, Mimi," he'd said. It wasn't the kind of compliment she usually got from a guy, but it was amazing how good it sounded. She'd found herself glancing casually around to see if Brad had heard, but of course he wasn't anywhere near.

"You know, I don't hurt so much tonight," she told Red.

"You're getting in shape," he said and added, "not that there was anything wrong with your shape to begin with. But it feels good, doesn't it?"

"It feels OK." If she turned her head just a little way she could watch Brad, watch his fingers twirling the stick, watch the way. . . .

"Five more days to go," Red said. "I'll be sorry when it's over."

"You told me you were weird the very first day," Mimi said absently. Brad was leaning toward Carol James, laughing at something she said.

Mimi got up on one elbow and pretended to stare into the fire. Carol had hair, black as Brad's, and she was good at things, like fording rivers and not whining when she slipped and got her feet wet. That was the kind of stuff Brad would admire. What if he were giving her the lizard look? So? What if he were? It certainly didn't matter to Mimi! She made herself turn back to Red.

"You scared about your solo?" Red asked.

"A bit. But not as much as I was at the beginning."

The solos were the testing-out part of camp where, for the last three days, each camper was left totally alone. They had to find their own food, make their own fires, live with their own thoughts. All things considered, the last one might be the hardest, Mimi decided. There were things she didn't want to think about or remember. Like the algebra test.

"Why did you do it, Mimi?" Mr. Sommers had asked.

"I don't know," Mimi said.

But she did know. Or at least, she knew now. Easier to cheat than to take time to study. Always easier to find the easy way. But up here there was no easy way. If something had to be done it had to be done and for the first time Mimi had a glimmering of the reasons behind her parents' decision to send her to Survival Camp.

"I'm planning on eating good," Red said, releasing her hand so he could give his stomach a comfortable pat. "Maybe I'll walk over and share my next rabbit with you."

"No," Mimi said quickly. "We're not. . .that's not the point of the solos." She lay back again with her face turned to the sky. She hadn't been kidding when she'd thought that the wilderness was turning her wacko. What was she doing, turning down free food, sounding all. . .all goody-goody, for Pete's sake?

"Brad said," she began and stopped, confused at the pleasure it gave her to say

Brad's name aloud. She put one arm over her eyes. "Well, anyway, Red, I don't think we should. They don't go in much for cheating up here." And Brad would look at me with that contemptuous expression, she thought, and I couldn't stand it. Not because he's special or anything. Just because, I guess, nobody likes to be despised. There's nothing wacko about that.

"OK," Red said. "I was just trying to make it easier for you."

"I know," Mimi smiled sideways at him. "Thanks, Red."

The stars were hidden by clouds by the time all the campers were under their blankets and the next two days threatened rain that didn't come.

The rain finally came on the night before the solos were to start, waking all of them from sleep, setting them to stumbling around in the light from their flashlights, and cutting sticks to make their rain shelters.

Mimi couldn't believe how snug and dry hers was when she finished it. She curled up inside with her plastic sheet over her, in case a few drops managed to get in, and there was a warming satisfaction in staring up at the roof of slatted sticks and grass that she'd made herself with no help from anyone. This is the way a coyote feels in its den, she thought contentedly, or a prairie dog in its burrow.

She was almost asleep again when a head popped under the shelter and a voice asked, "You OK in there?"

How did she know the voice so surely and so quickly? Her heart began a slow, hard hammering.

"Fine," she said.

"Looks like you did a pretty good job, Mimi."

"Oh." There was nothing more to say and no one to say it to. The head had gone.

"Pretty good job, Mimi," she whispered. If only it had been light enough to see him. Maybe he'd had the lizard look. Naw. The lizard look went with words like, "I love," or "You're fantastic." Not with "pretty good job, Mimi." But still. It could have been a semi-lizardy look, couldn't it? Sleep was slow to come, but her dreams were good and she came out of them reluctantly to the sound of the truck stopping in the clearing. Morning. The start of the solos.

A voice called, "come on, you lazy sods. Six-thirty a.m., time for the last big adventure."

The camp came groaningly awake.

The rain had stopped and the morning was cold and brightly colored. They scattered their shelters, piled up their belongings, and climbed into the back of the truck. Brad got in front with the driver.

Mimi stood wedged between Red and Harry. She ate a handful of dry oatmeal which stuck to the roof of her mouth and she wondered where all the sweet satisfaction of the night before had gone. This morning she felt grouchy and down. She told herself it had nothing to do with the fact that Brad had walked right past her toward the truck and hadn't spoken a single word. Not even a "sleep well in your 'nice-job' shelter?" Well, the heck with him anyway.

The truck bumped and rattled along, dropping a camper off every mile as Harry called off the names from his list. "See you in three days," he'd say. "Good luck. Remember, the nearest camper to you is only a mile away. Call if you get in trouble."

Mimi huddled her chin deep into the collar of her jacket and waited. When there were only five campers left she asked, "When do I go?"

U. S. 1991144

"You're next to last, Mimi," Harry said "Brad's at the end of the line. He wants you next to him in case..."

"In case what? In case I try to cheat?" Mimi asked quickly.

She felt her face getting warm. Why had she said that? A guilty conscience, and for once no need of one. She'd even turned down Red's offer of a visit.

"No," Harry said. "In case you need help. You're not exactly the strongest camper here, Mimi. He's put you between Red and himself. You might get another leg cramp."

Mimi looked at him suspiciously, but Harry's face was innocent.

After Red left, she was alone in the back of the truck. And when the truck stopped next, it was her turn to go.

Brad poked his head out of the cab window. "I'll be back in about three hours, Mimi. After that, if you need me, yell."

"I won't need you," Mimi said. She'd known it would take about three hours for Brad to go back with the driver and bring the truck again to the end of the line. But still, as she watched it turn and head back the way they'd come there was a sense of desolation. She made herself turn away and inspect her camp site.

There was plenty of firewood and she gathered enough to last all day and all night, too. It was cold, and the sky was dark. She built another shelter so she'd be ready if the rain did start. What if she heard the truck come back, and it stopped, and Brad said, "Pretty good job again there, Mimi?" But there was no engine sound to break the stillness.

There was pride in getting her fire started without using any of her three emergency matches. She patted the bulge of the match tin in her pocket. "I'm getting to be such a Davy Crockett I may never have to use you at all," she told them.

The ashcakes she cooked tasted pretty good, sprinkled with brown sugar. She sat, listening to the silence that was broken only by the occasional call of a bird and the drone of a solitary wasp.

The clouds dropped lower.

Mimi spread her plastic sheet on the floor of her shelter and crawled inside.

When the rain came it fell in a soft drizzle that misted the grass and the scrub. It smothered her fire. She brought a pile of her firewood under the shelter to keep it dry and make another fire easier to start. "See?" she said aloud. "I'm Mimi, and I'm coping just fine." She didn't know if she was talking to Brad, or to her brother, Dave, or to her parents or to herself. But the words held the ring of truth and they sounded good.

The soft monotony of the rain lulled her to sleep, and when something wakened her there was a moment's terrible uncertainty. Where was she? What had she heard? She sat up so quickly that her head bumped the roof and the shelter came down on her in a tumble of wet sticks and grass.

A coyote howled. Was that what she'd heard? No, there it was again. A voice. . .far, far away calling, "Help."

Coming from where? Where?

She stumbled out, still numb with sleep, feeling the rain heavy now, knowing that it was muffling the voice. She stopped wiping her wet face with a wet hand.

"Help! Help!"

Not from Brad's direction, which would have been east of her. Was Brad even back yet? She hadn't heard the truck passing. The voice wasn't from Red's direction either. That would have been west. But this was directly ahead, from the north.

"Help!"

Was it fainter now?

"Coming," she yelled. She slipped and slid on the wet grass. Pebbles rolled from under her feet.

Maybe she should have gone to see if Brad was back? Or called, at least?

She stopped and cupped a hand around her mouth. "Brad! Brad!" But she had to be really far away from him now. The mile, plus the extra distance she'd walked. If he was even back.

The other, faint voice came again and she forced herself on. She was so wet now that she was a part of the dripping desert. Water squelched from her shoes. Her jacket that had been light blue was black as ink.

The voice wasn't calling anymore. She stood in the rain, shivering with more than cold.

Someone groaned, so close that it scared her half to death. His bright red hair had rain-rusted to brown and his face was the color of the ashes in her drowned fire. One hand reached up to her and fell back.

"Red!" Mimi said, and she covered her mouth with her fist. Something was sticking out of his leg. A bone, white and shiny!

His head lifted. "Chasing rabbit," he said. "Fell. . . .down." His head dropped forward on his chest.

Mimi stared at him. I can't, she thought. I don't know what to do. Somebody, somebody. . .She wanted to run, to cry, to scream. But there was nobody to help him but her.

Her mind chased itself in circles. Should she leave him and go for help? But where, in what direction? She wasn't sure what way she'd turned, following his voice. Try to drag him? Not with that leg, that bone sticking out like that.

Red's eyes were open again. Suddenly and very distinctly he said, "I'm sorry, Mimi. The trouble with not being able to carry your own weight is that someone else has to carry it for you. Do you see?"

"Yes. Yes, Red," Mimi said and it seemed to her that she'd never heard so much wisdom in one sentence in her life. I need to think about that, for me, she thought. When I have time. "Don't worry, Red," she said. "I'm here."

His eyes stared beyond her and he said, "It hurts so much." Then his head dropped forward.

Mimi knelt beside him and put her ear to his chest, so frightened that all she could hear for a few seconds was the pumping of her own heart. Then she heard Red's too. "Don't worry, Red," she said again to his blank, white face. "Mimi's here."

She took off her jacket and spread it over him. Then she picked the matches out of the tin and shielded them from the rain while she inspected them. Were they still dry? They'd better be.

"Three fires," Harry had said. "The universal signal for danger." She'd light one close to Red so that he'd feel whatever warmth came from it.

The sobs came in spite of herself as she gathered the wood, and she found herself praying as her first match and then her second fizzled and died before the wood caught. But the third one lit, and she kindled the second two fires from the first.

"Come, someone, come," she begged.

Every few minutes she threw more pieces of wet wood on to the smoldering fires, and she felt the shudders shake and rattle through her body as the chill and wet reached down into her bones.

From time to time she stood and yelled, and she didn't know if it was rain that ran down her face or tears. She talked to Red too, though he gave no sign of hearing. She saw the day dying around her and knew that night was coming.

Twice she rose to a sound, joy bubbling in her that they'd been found. Both times it was wood shifting, or a small movement in the darkening desert.

And then, and then, a voice calling, "Mimi?" and the sound of her voice answering, splintering the silence.

"We're here. Oh, we're here."

And then she was running toward the sound, and the figure was coming to her out of the shadows.

"Brad! I thought you'd never find us, and it would be dark, and no one would see the smoke, and. . ."

"Sh!" His arms were tight around her,

holding her close till her shivering stopped. "Sh. I thought it was you, you in trouble."

He knelt by Red and his face was serious. "When I saw the smoke signal I brought the truck as far as I could get it in. It's down on the trail." He stood up. "I'll hike back down to it and call for help on the C.B. I think they'll probably have to send in a helicopter. Maybe not until morning."

"Will he. . . be all right?"

"It's a real bad break. But I think he'll be OK."

Relief made her dizzy. Red would be OK. No way not to believe Brad, ever.

"I'll get going," he said. "You stay with Red."

"Yes," Mimi said. He hadn't asked if she would or if she could, or if she could handle more of this. He knew she could. She was Mimi. Strong Mimi.

Brad touched her cheek with a thin brown finger and she didn't feel so strong anymore. "You did real fine, Mimi. You were terrific."

She caught her breath, The lizard look! The honest-to-goodness, unmistakable lizard look! The world had a new, pink glow.

She wondered if he knew that San Francisco State was one of the best Environmental Schools going. Sometime, later, before Survival Camp was over, she decided she'd tell him.